This book belongs to

_____

WALT DISNEY®

CHOOSE YOUR OWN ADVENTURE®

SNOW WHITE
in the Enchanted Forest
Story adapted by JIM RAZZI

Bantam  **Books**

TORONTO • NEW YORK • LONDON • SYDNEY • AUCKLAND

RL 2, 004–008

SNOW WHITE IN THE ENCHANTED FOREST

A Bantam Book / March 1985

CHOOSE YOUR OWN ADVENTURE® is a registered trade-mark of Bantam Books, Inc. Registered in U.S. Patent and Trademark Office and elsewhere.

*Concept: Edward Packard; Series Development:
R.A. Montgomery and Edward Packard.*

Library of Congress Cataloging in Publication Data

Razzi, Jim.
    Snow White in the enchanted forest.

    (Walt Disney choose your own adventure)
    Summary: The reader may choose from a variety of
adventures in the Enchanted Forest where the evil Queen is
searching for Snow White.
    1. Plot-your-own stories.   [1. Fairy tales.
2. Folklore—Germany.   3. Plot-your-own stories]
I. Schneewittchen.   II. Title.   III. Series.
PZ8.R22Sn   1985   398.2   84-20387
ISBN: 0-553-05401-5

Published simultaneously in the United States and Canada

Bantam Books are published by Bantam Books, Inc. Its trade-mark, consisting of the words "Bantam Books" and the portrayal of a rooster, is Registered in U.S. Patent and Trademark Office and in other countries. Marca Registrada. Bantam Books, Inc., 666 Fifth Avenue, New York, New York 10103.

PRINTED IN THE UNITED STATES OF AMERICA

DW   0 9 8 7 6 5 4 3 2 1

READ THIS FIRST!!!

Most books are about other people.

This book is about you—and Snow White.

Snow White is a beautiful Princess who lives in the cottage of the Seven Dwarfs.

Whatever happens in the story depends on what you decide to do.

Do not read this book from the first page through to the last page. Instead, start on page one and read until you come to your first choice. Decide what you want to do. Then turn to the page shown and see what happens.

When you come to the end of a story, go back and try another choice. Every choice leads to a new adventure.

While the Enchanted Forest is beautiful, it can hold many dangers. So be careful! If you are ready to start on your way, turn to page 1.

In a small kingdom nestled in a deep green valley   1
lives a Queen. She is very beautiful, but she is cruel and
wicked.

The Queen has a stepdaughter named Snow White,
who is even more beautiful than she. The Queen is so
jealous that she has plotted to have Snow White killed.
But Snow White has fled into the Enchanted Forest
and found shelter in the cottage of the Seven Dwarfs.

Calling on her magical powers, the angry Queen goes
after Snow White. She vows to find her and put an end
to her, once and for all!

You live in this small kingdom, and you have heard
the threats of the angry Queen.

One day, while riding on your horse, Hero, you lose
your way and find yourself in—the Enchanted Forest!

Turn to page 2.

2   Even though you're lost, you're not afraid.
Maybe you will meet Snow White!

   You ride Hero deeper and deeper into the forest. The place *does* seem enchanted.

   Suddenly you hear singing coming from just up ahead! You get off your horse and walk slowly forward. Just then, a twig snaps behind you. Someone is there! You spin around quickly but don't see a thing. What should you do?

If you want to see who's singing, turn to page 6.

If you decide to see who's behind you, turn to page 4.

You decide to find out who's behind you.

Out of the corner of your eye, you see a branch move. Something is hiding in the bushes!

Suddenly a little man darts out of them!

You grab him by the arm in surprise.

"Who are you?" you ask.

"My—my name is Bashful," he says. "I'm one of the Seven Dwarfs. Please let me go!"

"I won't hurt you," you say. "Why were you hiding?"

Go on to the next page.

"I was looking out for the evil Queen," he answers. "She knows Snow White is in this forest and she's after her!"

"Will you take me to see Snow White?" you ask.

"Yes," Bashful answers, "but please hurry. I know the evil Queen is near."

You are just about to go off with Bashful when you see a baby deer. It looks hurt. You want to help it, but you're not sure you have enough time.

If you stop to help the baby deer, turn to page 20.

If you go with Bashful right away, turn to page 10.

You want to see who's singing.

You keep on walking. In a small clearing, you see a little old woman carrying a basket of apples! As she sings, she looks curiously around. Is she lost too?

You walk over to her.

"Are you lost?" you ask kindly.

"Oh, dearie, you frightened me!" says the little old woman.

Go on to the next page.

"I'm awfully sorry," you say. "I was only trying to help."

The old woman gives you a funny little smile.

"Of course," she cackles. "You mean no harm."

Then a thoughtful look comes over her face. "Lost, you say? Yes, *hmm*, perhaps I am."

She looks slyly over at your horse. "A bit tired too!" she continues. "My poor old feet can't walk very far."

Go on to page 8.

8 You ask her what she is doing in the forest. To your surprise, she tells you she is looking for Snow White. The apples are a present for her.

"She is *so* kind to everyone," the old woman says. "I would like to be kind to her in return."

Maybe you should offer the woman a ride on your horse. She seems harmless, but you think there is something strange about her.

If you offer the old woman a ride, turn to page 14.

If you decide to go on your way, turn to page 18.

You and Bashful scramble onto Hero's back—you
don't want to meet the evil Queen!

"Where are the other dwarfs?" you ask, as you ride
along a tangled path.

"Just up ahead," says Bashful. "All except Sleepy—
he's with Snow White at the cottage."

Suddenly the five other dwarfs, Happy, Sneezy,
Grumpy, Dopey, and Doc, come running out of the
woods.

Go on to the next page.

"The Queen is near!" Doc yells.

"She's changed herself into a wild boar, and she's after us!" shouts Grumpy.

"We'd better . . . *achoo!* . . . warn Snow White and Sleepy," cries Sneezy.

But at that moment, a wild boar comes crashing through the woods. Your eyes grow wide. You have never *seen* a boar like this. It looks like something out of a nightmare!

Go on to page 12.

12 The huge beast glares at you and the dwarfs. Then it lowers its tusked head and charges.

But Hero is a brave stallion. He turns around and kicks the boar. *Whack!* The boar sails through the air and lands with a thud. It scampers to its feet with a howl and runs off.

"After it!" yells Bashful from behind you.

But you're not sure that's a good idea. The Queen might put a spell on you.

If you decide to listen to Bashful, turn to page 24.

If you don't want to chase the boar, turn to page 26.

14   You offer the old woman a ride on your horse.
"I would like to meet Snow White myself," you say.
"We can look for her together."

You ride a long way into the forest. At last you see a
cottage through the trees.
You leap off your horse and knock on the door.
You are greeted by Snow White herself!
"Hello," Snow White says sweetly.
"I'm so happy to see you, Princess," you say.
Just then, the old woman hobbles up beside you.
"Oh!" cries Snow White, a little frightened. "Who are
you?"

Go on to the next page.

"Don't worry," you say. "She's just an old woman who has brought you some apples."

The woman smiles and holds out a shiny red one in her bony hand.

"Yes, dearie," she says. "Take a bite and see how good it tastes."

Turn to page 17.

As soon as Snow White bites into the apple she falls to the ground. The apple must have been poisoned!

You turn to the old woman in horror. She's not there—but the wicked Queen is!

"Oh, no," you groan.

She points a finger at you. "Now it's *your* turn!"

Even though you want to help Snow White, you are afraid of the evil Queen's magic. You spring to your horse and ride until you come to a path that you know. You're not lost anymore!

But poor Snow White. What happened to *her?*

Turn to page 40.

"I'm sorry," you tell the old woman. "I must be on my way now. I can't help you look for Snow White."

"You *will* help me!" she shouts, her eyes bulging.

Now you are sure the old woman isn't who she seems to be. You walk back to your horse. Suddenly you hear a *piff!* You turn around. The old woman has disappeared, and in her place is the evil Queen!

Go on to the next page.

She was trying to trick you into helping her!

"Young fool!" she screams. "Help me find Snow White or I will turn you into a toad!"

You stand there bravely. You must protect Snow White.

"Bah!" the Queen says suddenly. "I haven't got time to waste on you now!" She disappears in a cloud of green smoke.

You breathe a sigh of relief. You certainly are glad the Queen was in a hurry!

The End

20 You stop to help the baby deer anyway.

Suddenly there is a puff of green smoke. *Zaff!* The deer is gone. And standing in its place is the evil Queen!

Bashful moans and scurries away.

"So, you want to be helpful, do you?" hisses the Queen. "Well, you shall. You shall help *me!*"

She points a slender finger at you. *Piff!*

The Queen has turned you into a raccoon!

Go on to the next page.

She sprinkles something on your fur.

"This potion is a special surprise just for Snow White. Now go into the forest and find her. She will want to pet you. And when she does, my potion will seep into her skin. It will make her forget who she is and where she is. Then I will catch her easily."

The Queen laughs.

You look around wildly. All you want to do is run as far away as you can from the evil Queen.

Turn to page 23.

You run and run until your four legs hurt.

All at once, you spy a cottage through the trees. You scamper up to it curiously—and Snow White herself comes out the door!

"What a darling little raccoon!" Snow White cries when she sees you. "May I pet you?"

You can't speak, and the Queen's spell won't let you run away. What should you do?

Maybe you can frighten Snow White by growling at her. Or maybe you can shiver and act sick. That might frighten her, too.

If you growl at Snow White, turn to page 36.

If you shiver and act sick, turn to page 28.

You decide to listen to Bashful. He clings to your back as you set off at full gallop.

The chase leads through the woods and up to a high, steep cliff. You corner the wild beast near the edge of the cliff.

Suddenly there is a blinding flash of light—*zap!* The evil Queen stands before you!

At that moment, Hero rears up on his hind legs and forces her to the very edge of the cliff.

Go on to the next page.

The Queen is taken by surprise. She stumbles back and falls over the cliff!

"Hooray!" yells Bashful. "Snow White is safe at last! The Queen can never harm her again."

"Let's all go back to the cottage and tell Snow White the good news!" cries Bashful.

"All right!" you say.

Getting lost in the Enchanted Forest is turning out to be very exciting!

The End

You don't want to chase the boar. Instead, you ask the dwarfs if you could meet Snow White now.

They seem to take a long time making up their minds.

Bashful starts to fidget. "We have wasted too much time already," he says. "Let's go!"

The dwarfs finally agree. They march off into the woods and beckon you to follow.

After you have traveled a bit, Bashful points to a little cottage in a clearing. "We're home!" he shouts.

Go on to the next page.

As you near the cottage, Sleepy runs up to you. He's crying!

"Sleepy, what's wrong?" asks Doc.

"The wicked Queen was just here," sobs Sleepy, "disguised as an old woman. She gave Snow White a poisoned apple and now I can't wake her up! The Queen has put a spell on her, and it's all my fault!"

"No, it's my fault," you say. "I should have gone after the wild boar. But it's too late now."

The End

You decide to shiver and act sick.

But instead of being frightened, Snow White runs over to you.

You try to run away, but you can't.

"Poor little thing," Snow White murmurs as she strokes your fur.

"Oh!" she cries suddenly. "I'm getting dizzy. Where am I? *Who* am I?"

She has lost her memory!

Go on to the next page.

Snow White runs into the woods. You follow her. Now that you've done the Queen's bidding, you're yourself again.

"Wait for me!" you shout.

Snow White stops and turns to look at you. "Who are you?" she asks.

You tell her you want to be her friend.

"I do need a friend," she says.

Then you walk along until, with a sinking heart, you realize that you are now *both* lost in the Enchanted Forest.

Go on to page 30.

30   Suddenly you come upon a thick grove of large black trees. Their trunks are twisted and gnarled. They look very scary. But the grove might lead to a way out of the forest. You decide to take a chance and go through it.

"Let's tiptoe through the grove," you whisper to Snow White. "We don't want anything that might be in there to hear us."

Or maybe it would be better just to run.

If you tiptoe through the grove, turn to page 32.

If you run through the grove, turn to page 38.

You tiptoe through the grove.

Out of nowhere, a funny little green fairy appears before you. "Who's sneaking around in my grove?" she asks angrily.

Quickly you explain that you weren't sneaking anywhere. You tell her all about what happened and how Snow White lost her memory.

"Well, fiddlesticks!" cries the fairy. "I can give her back her memory."

Go on to the next page.

"You can?" you say.

In answer, the green fairy waves her magic wand. Snow White's face lights up. "What am I doing here?" she asks. "Where are the Seven Dwarfs?"

She's got her memory back!

The green fairy turns to you and waves her wand again. "But now I'm afraid you will have to lose yours! You must forget the Enchanted Forest."

Turn to page 35.

You find yourself back on your horse!

Where are you? . . . Oh, *now* you remember. . . . You're out riding your horse, Hero. But you feel strange. Have you been sleeping in the saddle?

You look up at the sun. It's almost ready to set. What's going on? You can't even remember what you did all day!

"Oh, well," you sigh. You probably did something very boring that you'd rather *forget*!

The End

36 You growl at Snow White.
She backs away. It was a good idea!
Just then Bashful and the other dwarfs run up.
"Grab that raccoon!" Bashful yells.
All the dwarfs pounce on you at once.
Bashful tells everyone about the Queen's spell. He had been watching from the bushes.
"Poor little thing," says Snow White. "It must be thirsty." She takes a ladle of water from a bucket.

Go on to the next page.

"Drink, little raccoon," she says kindly.

Zap! There's a blinding flash. You're *you* again. Snow White's kindness has broken the spell!

After you explain that you meant no harm, Snow White asks if you would like to stay with her and the Seven Dwarfs for a while. "We can have a party!" she says.

You smile. You know you will enjoy your visit in the Enchanted Forest very much!

The End

You both start running through the grove.

Suddenly a tree tries to grab you with its branches. It's alive!

"Oh!" screams Snow White.

Soon every tree is trying to grab you and Snow White. Evil wood-spirits live in the trees, and your noise has awakened them!

Before you know it, you and Snow White are trapped in a cage of branches.

Go on to the next page.

Everything grows still.

You hear someone coming. It's the Queen!

"So, my little friends," she snarls. "The black trees have caught you for me. How kind of them."

You struggle to escape from the trees, but it's no use. Your only hope is that the Seven Dwarfs will come looking for you and Snow White before the Queen works her evil magic. But will they reach you in time? You certainly hope so.

The End

40　　A few weeks later you return to the Enchanted Forest. This time you know your way. You are still afraid of the evil Queen, but you *have* to find out what happened to Snow White.

On your way, you meet another rider. He tells you his name is Prince Charming.

"I am looking for a beautiful Princess," he says. "I met her once, long ago, and we fell in love. Now I have heard about a Princess who lies asleep in the forest. I wonder if she and my Princess are the same?"

Turn to page 43.

"I know where this Princess sleeps!" you cry.

You and the Prince gallop to a small meadow near the cottage of the Seven Dwarfs. There, on a flowered mound, lies Snow White.

The Prince gets off his horse and goes to her.

"It is my Princess," he says sadly. Bending over, he kisses her tenderly.

Snow White's eyes flutter open. She's awake! Love's First Kiss has broken the Queen's spell.

You are glad you came back to the Enchanted Forest. This time the path has led to a happy

. . . Ending!